The Canterville Ghost

Oscar Wilde

Published by

MAPLE PRESS PRIVATE LIMITED
office: A-63, Sector 58, Noida 201301, U.P., India
phone: +91 120 455 3581, 455 3583
email: info@maplepress.co.in
website: www.maplepress.co.in

Reprint 2021 in India

ISBN: 978-93-50330-58-6

Contents

Chapter 1

When Mr. Hiram B. Otis, the American Minister, bought Canterville Chase, every one told him he was doing a very foolish thing, as there was no doubt at all that the place was haunted. Indeed, Lord Canterville himself, who was a man of the most punctilious honour, had felt it his duty to mention the fact to Mr. Otis when they came to discuss terms.

"We have not cared to live in the place ourselves," said Lord Canterville, "since my grandaunt, the Dowager Duchess of Bolton, was frightened into a fit, from which she never really recovered, by two skeleton hands being placed on her shoulders as she was dressing for dinner, and I feel bound to tell you, Mr. Otis, that the ghost has been seen by several living members of my family, as well as by the rector of the parish, the Rev. Augustus Dampier, who is a Fellow of King's College, Cambridge. After the unfortunate accident to the Duchess, none of our younger servants would stay with us, and Lady Canterville often got very little sleep at night, in consequence of the mysterious noises that came from the corridor and the library."

"My Lord," answered the Minister, "I will take the furniture and the ghost at a valuation. I have come from a modern country, where we have everything that money can buy; and with all our spry young fellows painting the Old World red, and carrying off your best actors and prima-donnas, I reckon that if there were such a thing as a ghost in Europe, we'd have it at home in a very short time in one of our public museums, or on the road as a show."

"I fear that the ghost exists," said Lord Canterville, smiling, "though it may have resisted the overtures of your enterprising impresarios. It has been well known for three centuries, since 1584 in fact, and always makes its appearance before the death of any member of our family."

"Well, so does the family doctor for that matter, Lord Canterville. But there is no such thing, sir, as a ghost, and I guess the laws of Nature are not going to be suspended for the British aristocracy."

"You are certainly very natural in America," answered Lord Canterville, who did not quite understand Mr. Otis's last observation, "and if you don't mind a ghost in the house, it is all right. Only you must remember I warned you."

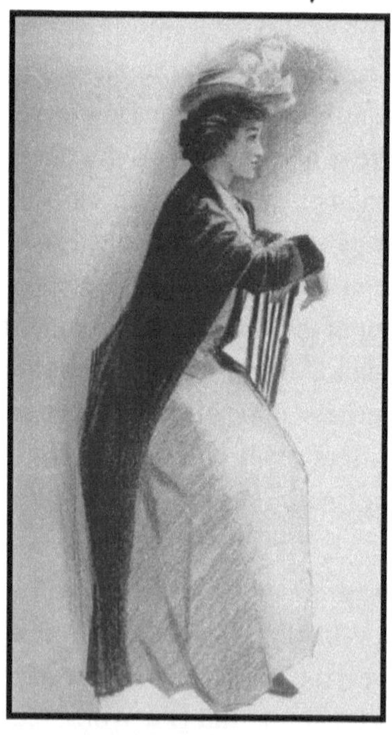

MISS VIRGINIA E. OTIS

A few weeks after this, the purchase was concluded, and at the close of the season the Minister and his family went down to Canterville Chase. Mrs. Otis, who, as Miss Lucretia R. Tappan, of West 53d Street, had been a celebrated New York belle, was now a very handsome, middle-aged woman, with fine eyes, and a superb profile. Many American ladies on leaving their native land adopt an appearance of chronic ill-health, under the impression that it is a form of European refinement, but Mrs. Otis had never fallen into this error. She had a magnificent constitution, and a really wonderful amount of animal spirits. Indeed, in many respects, she was quite English, and was an excellent example of the fact that we have really everything in common with America nowadays, except, of course, language. Her eldest son, christened Washington by his parents in a moment of patriotism, which he never ceased to regret, was a fair-haired, rather good-looking young man, who had qualified himself for American diplomacy by leading the German at the Newport Casino for three successive seasons, and even in London was well known as an excellent dancer. Gardenias and the peerage were his only weaknesses. Otherwise he was extremely sensible. Miss Virginia E. Otis was a little girl of fifteen, lithe and lovely as a fawn, and with a fine freedom in her large blue eyes. She was a wonderful Amazon, and had once raced old Lord Bilton on her pony twice round the park, winning by a length and a half, just in front of the Achilles statue, to the huge delight of the young Duke of Cheshire, who proposed for her on the spot, and was sent back to Eton that very night by his guardians, in floods of tears. After Virginia came the twins, who were usually called "The Star and Stripes," as they were always getting swished. They were delightful boys, and, with the exception of the worthy Minister, the only true republicans of the family.

"HAD ONCE RACED OLD LORD BILTON ON HER PONY"

As Canterville Chase is seven miles from Ascot, the nearest railway station, Mr. Otis had telegraphed for a waggonette to meet them, and they started on their drive in high spirits. It was a lovely July evening, and the air was delicate with the scent of the pinewoods. Now and then they heard a wood-pigeon brooding over its own sweet voice, or saw, deep in the rustling fern, the burnished breast of the pheasant. Little squirrels peered at them from the beech-trees as they went by, and the rabbits scudded away through the brushwood and over the mossy knolls, with their white tails in the air. As they entered the avenue of Canterville Chase, however, the sky became suddenly overcast with clouds, a curious stillness seemed to hold the atmosphere, a great flight of rooks passed silently over their heads, and, before they reached the house, some big drops of rain had fallen.

Standing on the steps to receive them was an old woman, neatly dressed in black silk, with a white cap and apron. This was

Mrs. Umney, the housekeeper, whom Mrs. Otis, at Lady Canterville's earnest request, had consented to keep in her former position. She made them each a low curtsey as they alighted, and said in a quaint, old-fashioned manner, "I bid you welcome to Canterville Chase." Following her, they passed through the fine Tudor hall into the library, a long, low room, panelled in black oak, at the end of which was a large stained glass window. Here they found tea laid out for them, and, after taking off their wraps, they sat down and began to look round, while Mrs. Umney waited on them.

Suddenly Mrs. Otis caught sight of a dull red stain on the floor just by the fireplace, and, quite unconscious of what it really signified, said to Mrs. Umney, "I am afraid something has been spilt there."

"Yes, madam," replied the old housekeeper in a low voice, "blood has been spilt on that spot."

"BLOOD HAS BEEN SPILLED ON THAT SPOT"

"How horrid!" cried Mrs. Otis; "I don't at all care for blood-stains in a sitting-room. It must be removed at once."

The old woman smiled, and answered in the same low, mysterious voice, "It is the blood of Lady Eleanore de Canterville, who was murdered on that very spot by her own husband, Sir Simon de Canterville, in 1575. Sir Simon survived her nine years, and disappeared suddenly under very mysterious circumstances. His body has never been discovered, but his guilty spirit still haunts the Chase. The blood-stain has been much admired by tourists and others, and cannot be removed."

"That is all nonsense," cried Washington Otis; "Pinkerton's Champion Stain Remover and Paragon Detergent will clean it up in no time," and before the terrified housekeeper could interfere, he had fallen upon his knees, and was rapidly scouring the floor with a small stick of what looked like a black cosmetic. In a few moments no trace of the blood-stain could be seen.

"I knew Pinkerton would do it," he exclaimed, triumphantly, as he looked round at his admiring family; but no sooner had he said these words than a terrible flash of lightning lit up the sombre room, a fearful peal of thunder made them all start to their feet, and Mrs. Umney fainted.

"What a monstrous climate!" said the American Minister, calmly, as he lit a long cheroot. "I guess the old country is so overpopulated that they have not enough decent weather for everybody. I have always been of opinion that emigration is the only thing for England."

"My dear Hiram," cried Mrs. Otis, "what can we do with a woman who faints?"

"Charge it to her like breakages," answered the Minister; "she won't faint after that;" and in a few moments Mrs. Umney certainly came to. There was no doubt, however, that she was extremely upset, and she sternly warned Mr. Otis to beware of some trouble coming to the house.

"I have seen things with my own eyes, sir," she said, "that would make any Christian's hair stand on end, and many and many a night I have not closed my eyes in sleep for the awful things that are done here." Mr. Otis, however, and his wife warmly assured the honest soul that they were not afraid of ghosts, and, after invoking the blessings of Providence on her new master and mistress, and making arrangements for an increase of salary, the old housekeeper tottered off to her own room.

THINK AND INK...

Questions:

1. What opinion do you form about Lord Canterville who felt it his duty to tell Mr. Otis about the haunted hosue?

2. Why was Mr. Otis eager to buy the house?

3. What contrasting picture of the American and the British did Mr. Otis present in his conversation?

4. 'Mrs. Otis had never fallen into this error' - what error does Mr. Otis refer to, and why had she not fallen into that?

5. Do you think the atmosphere presented some ghostliness as the Otis family arrived at the Canterville Chase? How?

6. Does the bloodstain on the floor disturb the Otis family in any way? Why/why not?

Text based questions:

1. Why was buying the Canterville Chase a foolish thing? Was Mr.Otis a fool then? If not, give reasons.

2. What type of a person was Lord Canterville?

3. How was the Lord so sure about the presence of ghost?

4. How did Mr. Otis convince Lord Canterville of his decision to buy the house?

5. What do you understand by Mr. Otis's comment, 'the laws of Nature are not going to be suspended for the British aristrocracy'?

6. Describe the family of Mr. Otis.

7. What contrasting scene does the Otis family find in their journey from the station to Canterville Chase?

8. From her reaction to the bloodstain, what does Mrs. Otis prove?

9. What is the story about Sir, Simon de Canterville as narrated by Mrs. Umney?

10. How does the ghost make its presence felt when Mr. Otis wiped the bloodstain?

11. Why was Mrs. Umney extremely upset?

12. Throw light on how the author prepares the readers for the presence of ghost at the Canterville Chase?

Vocabulary

1. Haunted – visited by ghosts

2. Punctilious – careful

3. Terms – agreement

4. Fit – unconscious

5. Rector – cleric in charge of a church

6. Parish – a place having its own church

7. Unfortunate – unlucky

8. Duchess – wife of a duke

9. Valuation – value

10. Spry – active, lively

11. Old World red – making Britain active

12. Carrying off – (here) impress

13. Prima – donnas – female singers in a opera

14. Reckon – think

15. Resisted – opposed

16. Overtures – approaches

17. Enterprising – creative

18. Impresarios – organisers,directors

19. Suspended – stopped

20. Aristrocracy – nobles

21. Celebrated – popular

22. Belle – lady

23. Profile – appearance

24. Chronic – serious

25. Ill-health – disease, illness

26. Refinement – sophistication

27. Magnificent – wonderful

28. Constitution – health

29. Animal spirits – vital strengths

30. Christened – named

31. Ceased – stopped

32. Diplomacy – the conduct for international relationships

33. Casino – gambling place

34. Gardenias – flowers

35. Peerage – of equal position

36. Lithe – flexible

37. Fawn – baby deer

38. Amazon – tall and powerful

39. Achilles – a Greek hero

40. Swished – together

41. Republicans – supporters of the Republican party

42. Waggonette – a wagon

43. High spirits – excitement

44. Rustling – crackling

45. Fern – leaf

46. Burnished – glossy

47. Pheasant – a bird

48. Peered – looked

49. Scudded – ran

50. Mossy knolls – small hills with moss

51. Overcast – cloudy

52. Stillness – silence

53. Rook – a bird

54. Earnest – serious

55. Consented – agreed

56. Former – previous

57. Curtsy – bow

58. Alighted – got down

59. Quaint – appealing

60. Wraps – shawls

61. Stain – blot

62. Horrid – horrible

63. Scouring – wiping

64. Triumphantly – victoriously

65. Sombre – sad

66. Peal – sound

67. Cheroot – cigar

68. Charge... breakages – charge as if for broken items

69. Sternly – seriously

70. Awful – dreadful

71. Providence – God

72. Tottered – stumble

Chapter 2

The storm raged fiercely all that night, but nothing of particular note occurred. The next morning, however, when they came down to breakfast, they found the terrible stain of blood once again on the floor. "I don't think it can be the fault of the Paragon Detergent," said Washington, "for I have tried it with everything. It must be the ghost." He accordingly rubbed out the stain a second time, but the second morning it appeared again. The third morning also it was there, though the library had been locked up at night by Mr. Otis himself, and the key carried up-stairs. The whole family were now quite interested; Mr. Otis began to suspect that he had been too dogmatic in his denial of the existence of ghosts, Mrs. Otis expressed her intention of joining the Psychical Society, and Washington prepared a long letter to Messrs. Myers and Podmore on the subject of the Permanence of Sanguineous Stains when connected with Crime. That night all doubts about the objective existence of phantasmata were removed for ever.

The day had been warm and sunny; and, in the cool of the evening, the whole family went out to drive. They did not return home till nine o'clock, when they had a light supper. The conversation in no way turned upon ghosts, so there were not even those primary conditions of receptive expectations which so often precede the presentation of psychical phenomena. The subjects discussed, as I have since learned from Mr. Otis, were merely such as form the ordinary conversation of cultured Americans of the better class, such as the immense superiority of Miss Fanny Devonport over Sarah Bernhardt as an actress; the difficulty of obtaining green corn, buckwheat cakes, and hominy, even in the best English houses; the importance of Boston in the development of the world-soul; the advantages of the baggage-check system in railway travelling; and the sweetness of the New York accent as compared to the London drawl. No mention at all was made of the supernatural, nor was Sir Simon de Canterville alluded to in any way. At eleven o'clock the family retired, and by half-past all the lights were out. Some time after, Mr. Otis was awakened by a curious noise in the corridor, outside his room. It sounded like the clank of metal, and seemed to be coming nearer every moment. He got up at once, struck a match, and looked at the time. It was exactly one o'clock. He was quite calm, and felt his pulse, which was not at all feverish. The strange noise still continued, and with it he heard distinctly the sound of footsteps. He put on his slippers, took a small oblong phial out of his dressing-case, and opened the door. Right in front of him he saw, in the wan moonlight, an old man of terrible aspect. His eyes were as red burning coals; long grey hair fell over his shoulders in matted coils; his garments, which were of antique cut, were soiled and ragged, and from his wrists and ankles hung heavy manacles and rusty gyves.

"My dear sir," said Mr. Otis, "I really must insist on your oiling those chains, and have brought you for that purpose a small bottle of the Tammany Rising Sun Lubricator. It is said to be completely efficacious upon one application, and there are several testimonials to that effect on the wrapper from some of our most eminent native divines. I shall leave it here for you by the bedroom candles, and will be happy to supply you with more, should you require it." With these words the United States Minister laid the bottle down on a marble table, and, closing his door, retired to rest.

"I REALLY MUST INSIST ON YOUR OILING THOSE CHAINS"

For a moment the Canterville ghost stood quite motionless in natural indignation; then, dashing the bottle violently upon the polished floor, he fled down the corridor, uttering hollow groans, and emitting a ghastly green light. Just, however, as he reached the top of the great oak staircase, a door was flung open, two little white-robed figures appeared, and a large pillow whizzed past his head! There was evidently no time to be lost, so, hastily adopting the Fourth dimension of Space as a means of escape, he vanished through the wainscoting, and the house became quite quiet.

On reaching a small secret chamber in the left wing, he leaned up against a moonbeam to recover his breath, and began to try and realize his position. Never, in a brilliant and uninterrupted career of three hundred years, had he been so grossly insulted. He thought of the Dowager Duchess, whom he had frightened into a fit as she stood before the glass in her lace and diamonds; of the four housemaids, who had gone into hysterics when he merely grinned at them through the curtains on one of the spare bedrooms; of the rector of the parish, whose candle he had blown out as he was coming late one night from the library, and who had been under the care of Sir William Gull ever since, a perfect martyr to nervous disorders; and of old Madame de Tremouillac, who, having wakened up one morning early and seen a skeleton seated in an armchair by the fire reading her diary, had been confined to her bed for six weeks with an attack of brain fever, and, on her recovery, had become reconciled to the Church, and broken off her connection with that notorious sceptic, Monsieur de Voltaire. He remembered the terrible night when the wicked Lord Canterville was found choking in his dressing-room, with the knave of diamonds half-way down his throat, and confessed, just before he died, that he had cheated Charles James Fox out of £50,000 at Crockford's by means of that very card, and swore that the ghost had made him swallow it. All his great achievements came back to him again, from the butler who had shot himself in the pantry because he had seen a green hand tapping at the window-pane, to the beautiful Lady Stutfield, who was always obliged to wear a black velvet band round her throat to hide the mark of five fingers burnt upon her white skin, and who drowned herself at last in the carp-pond at the end of the

King's Walk. With the enthusiastic egotism of the true artist, he went over his most celebrated performances, and smiled bitterly to himself as he recalled to mind his last appearance as "Red Reuben, or the Strangled Babe," his debut as "Guant Gibeon, the Blood-sucker of Bexley Moor," and the furore he had excited one lovely June evening by merely playing ninepins with his own bones upon the lawn-tennis ground. And after all this some wretched modern Americans were to come and offer him the Rising Sun Lubricator, and throw pillows at his head! It was quite unbearable. Besides, no ghost in history had ever been treated in this manner. Accordingly, he determined to have vengeance, and remained till daylight in an attitude of deep thought.

THINK AND INK...

Questions :

1. Why did the Otis family go out?
2. Why did they not discuss the ghost during supper?
3. Does the fact that the family did not discuss about ghosts prove their approval of its presence? Does it shake their confidence?
4. Was it because of their doubt about the presence of ghost that they avoided the topic?
5. How does Mr. Otis prepare himself for the encounter of the ghost?
6. How does the bloodstain reappear?
7. Does the bloodstain somewhat shake the confidence of Mr. Otis's family?
8. What opinion do you form about Mr. Otis's reaction at the sound of the metal?
9. What gives the Otis's children the boldness to face the ghost? Is it due to their up bringing? Or has it got anything to do with their background?

Text-based Questions:

1. Why does Mrs. Otis want to join the psychical society?
2. What topics were discussed by the family during supper? Could this be a deliberate move to avoid thoughts of ghosts?
3. How was the old ghost looking?
4. What did Mr. Otis advise to the ghost? What did the act suggest about Otis?
5. Why was the ghost angry?
6. Why did the ghost want to escape from the scene?
7. What were the achievements of the ghost in his career of three hundred years?
8. What did the butler do on seeing the ghost?

Vocabulary :

1. Fiercely – strongly
2. Dogmatic – strict
3. Denial – disapproval
4. Sanguineous – blood red
5. Objective – detached
6. Phantasmata – a perception, an illusion
7. Receptive – acceptable
8. Precede – go before
9. Phenomena – idea
10. Hominy – oats
11. Drawl – to speak with lengthened vowels
12. Alluded – referred
13. Retired – went to bed
14. Clank – sound
15. Distinctly – clearly
16. Phial – bottle
17. Wan – pale
18. Aspect – feature
19. Matted coils – entwined
20. Antique – old fashioned
21. Soiled – dirty
22. Ragged – torn
23. Manacles – chains
24. Gyves – fetters
25. Insist – compel
26. Lubricator – oil

27. Efficacious – effective
28. Testimonials – proofs
29. Eminent – well-known
30. Divines – clerics
31. Indignation – anger
32. Groans – cries
33. Emitting – giving out
34. Ghastly – terrible
35. Whizzed – zoomed
36. Fourth Dimension of Space – high speed
37. Grossly – totally
38. Hysterics – a mental disorder
39. Grinned – smiled
40. Reconciled – accepted
41. Notorious – infamous
42. Sceptic – disbeliever
43. Choking – difficulty in breathing
44. Knave of diamonds – a method of playing cards
45. Obliged – compelled
46. Egotism – self-pride
47. Furore – uproar
48. Vengeance – take revenge

Chapter 3

The next morning, when the Otis family met at breakfast, they discussed the ghost at some length. The United States Minister was naturally a little annoyed to find that his present had not been accepted. "I have no wish," he said, "to do the ghost any personal injury, and I must say that, considering the length of time he has been in the house, I don't think it is at all polite to throw pillows at him,"- - a very just remark, at which, I am sorry to say, the twins burst into shouts of laughter. "Upon the other hand," he continued, "if he really declines to use the Rising Sun Lubricator, we shall have to take his chains from him. It would be quite impossible to sleep, with such a noise going on outside the bedrooms."

For the rest of the week, however, they were undisturbed, the only thing that excited any attention being the continual renewal of the blood-stain on the library floor. This certainly was very strange, as the door was always locked at night by Mr. Otis, and the windows kept closely barred. The chameleon-like colour, also, of the stain excited a good deal of comment. Some mornings it was a dull (almost Indian) red, then it would be vermilion, then a rich purple, and once when they came down for family prayers, according to the simple rites of the Free American Reformed Episcopalian Church, they found it a bright emerald-green. These kaleidoscopic changes naturally amused the party very much, and bets on the subject were freely made every evening. The only person who did not enter into the joke was little Virginia, who, for some unexplained reason, was always a good deal distressed at the sight of the blood-stain, and very nearly cried the morning it was emerald-green.

The second appearance of the ghost was on Sunday night. Shortly after they had gone to bed they were suddenly alarmed by a fearful crash in the hall. Rushing down-stairs, they found that a large suit of old armour had become detached from its stand, and had fallen on the stone floor, while seated in a high-backed chair was the Canterville ghost, rubbing his knees with an expression of acute agony on his face. The twins, having brought their

"THE TWINS ... AT ONCE DISCHARGED TWO PELLETS ON HIM"

pea-shooters with them, at once discharged two pellets on him, with that accuracy of aim which can only be attained by long and careful practice on a writing-master, while the United States Minister covered him with his revolver, and called upon him, in accordance with Californian etiquette, to hold up his hands! The ghost started up with a wild shriek of rage, and swept through them like a mist, extinguishing Washington Otis's candle as he passed, and so leaving them all in total darkness. On reaching the top of the staircase he recovered himself, and determined to give his celebrated peal of demoniac laughter. This he had on more than one occasion found extremely useful. It was said to have turned Lord Raker's wig grey in a single night, and had certainly made three of Lady Canterville's French governesses give warning before their month was up. He accordingly laughed his most horrible laugh, till the old vaulted roof rang and rang again, but hardly had the fearful echo died away when a door opened, and Mrs. Otis came out in a light blue dressing-gown. "I am afraid you are far from well," she said, "and have brought you a bottle of Doctor Dobell's tincture. If it is indigestion, you will find it a most excellent remedy." The ghost glared at her in fury, and began at once to make preparations for turning himself into a large black dog, an accomplishment for which he was justly renowned, and to which the family doctor always attributed the permanent idiocy of Lord Canterville's uncle, the Hon. Thomas Horton. The sound of approaching footsteps, however, made him hesitate in his fell purpose, so he contented himself with becoming faintly phosphorescent, and vanished with a deep churchyard groan, just as the twins had come up to him.

On reaching his room he entirely broke down, and became a prey to the most violent agitation. The vulgarity of the twins, and the gross materialism of Mrs. Otis, were naturally extremely annoying, but what really distressed him most was that he had been unable to wear the suit of mail. He had hoped that even modern Americans would be thrilled by the sight of a Spectre in armour, if for no more sensible reason, at least out of respect for their natural poet Longfellow, over whose graceful and attractive poetry he himself had whiled away many a weary hour when the Cantervilles were up in town. Besides it was his own suit. He had worn it with great success at the Kenilworth tournament, and had been highly complimented on it by no less a person than the Virgin Queen herself. Yet when he had put it on, he had been completely overpowered by the weight of the huge breastplate and steel casque, and had fallen heavily on the stone pavement, barking both his knees severely, and bruising the knuckles of his right hand.

For some days after this he was extremely ill, and hardly stirred out of his room at all, except to keep the blood-stain in proper repair. However, by taking great care of himself, he recovered, and resolved to make a third attempt to frighten the United States Minister and his family. He selected Friday, August 17th, for his appearance, and spent most of that day in looking over his wardrobe, ultimately deciding in favour of a large slouched hat with a red feather, a winding-sheet frilled at the wrists and neck, and a rusty dagger. Towards evening a violent storm of rain came on, and the wind was so high that all the windows and doors in the old house shook and rattled. In fact, it was just such weather as he loved. His plan of action was this. He was to make his way quietly to Washington Otis's room, gibber at him from the foot of the bed, and stab himself three times in the throat to the sound of low music. He bore Washington a special grudge, being quite aware that it was he who was in the habit of removing the famous Canterville blood-stain by means of Pinkerton's Paragon Detergent. Having reduced the reckless and foolhardy youth to a condition of abject terror, he was then to proceed to the room occupied by the United States Minister and his wife, and there to place a clammy hand on Mrs. Otis's forehead, while he hissed into her trembling husband's ear the awful secrets of the charnel-house. With regard to little Virginia, he had not quite made up his mind. She had never insulted him in any way, and was pretty and gentle. A few hollow groans from the wardrobe, he thought, would be more than sufficient, or, if that failed to wake her, he might grabble at the counterpane with palsy-twitching fingers. As for the twins, he was quite determined to teach them a lesson. The first thing to be done was, of course, to sit upon their chests, so as to produce the stifling sensation of nightmare. Then, as their beds were quite close to each other, to stand between them in the form of a green, icy-cold corpse, till they became paralyzed with fear, and finally, to throw off the winding-sheet, and crawl round the room, with white, bleached bones and one rolling eyeball, in the character of "Dumb Daniel, or the Suicide's Skeleton," a role in which he had on more than one occasion produced a great effect, and which he considered quite equal to his famous part of "Martin the Maniac, or the Masked Mystery."

At half-past ten he heard the family going to bed. For some time he was disturbed by wild shrieks of laughter from the twins, who, with the light-hearted gaiety of schoolboys, were evidently amusing themselves before they retired to rest, but at a quarter-past eleven all was still, and, as midnight sounded, he sallied forth. The owl beat against the window-panes, the raven croaked from the old yew-tree, and the wind wandered moaning round the house like a lost soul; but the Otis family slept unconscious of their doom, and high above the rain and storm he could hear the steady snoring of the Minister for the United States. He stepped stealthily out of the wainscoting, with an evil smile on his cruel, wrinkled mouth, and the moon hid her face in a cloud as he stole past the great oriel window, where his own arms and those of his murdered wife were blazoned in azure and gold. On and on he glided, like an evil shadow, the very darkness seeming to loathe him as he passed. Once he thought he heard something call, and stopped; but it was only the baying of a dog from the Red Farm, and he went on, muttering strange sixteenth-century curses, and ever and anon brandishing the rusty dagger in the midnight air. Finally he reached the corner of the passage that led to luckless Washington's room. For a moment he paused there, the wind blowing his long grey locks about his head, and twisting into grotesque and fantastic folds the nameless horror of the dead man's shroud. Then the clock struck the quarter, and he felt the time was come. He chuckled to himself, and turned the corner; but no sooner had he done so than, with a piteous wail of terror, he fell back, and hid his blanched face in his long, bony hands. Right in front of him was standing a horrible spectre, motionless as a carven image, and monstrous as a madman's dream! Its head was bald and burnished; its face round, and fat, and white; and hideous laughter seemed to have writhed its features into an eternal grin. From the eyes streamed rays of scarlet light, the mouth was a wide well of fire, and a hideous garment, like to his own, swathed with its silent snows the Titan form. On its breast was a placard with strange writing in antique characters, some scroll of shame it seemed, some record of wild sins, some awful calendar of crime, and, with its right hand, it bore aloft a falchion of gleaming steel.

"ITS HEAD WAS BALD AND BURNISHED"

Never having seen a ghost before, he naturally was terribly frightened, and, after a second hasty glance at the awful phantom, he fled back to his room, tripping up in his long winding-sheet as he sped down the corridor, and finally dropping the rusty dagger into the Minister's jack-boots, where it was found in the morning by the butler. Once in the privacy of his own apartment, he flung himself down on a small pallet-bed, and hid his face under the clothes. After a time, however, the brave old Canterville spirit asserted itself, and he determined to go and speak to the other ghost as soon as it was daylight. Accordingly, just as the dawn was touching the hills with silver, he returned towards the spot where he had first laid eyes on the grisly phantom, feeling that, after all, two ghosts were better than one, and that, by the aid of his new friend, he might safely grapple with the twins. On reaching the spot, however, a terrible sight met his gaze. Something had evidently happened to the spectre, for the light had entirely faded from its hollow eyes, the gleaming falchion had fallen from its hand, and it was leaning up against the wall in a strained and uncomfortable attitude. He rushed forward and seized it in his arms, when, to his horror, the head slipped off and rolled on the floor, the body assumed a recumbent posture, and he found himself clasping a white dimity bed-curtain, with a sweeping-brush, a kitchen cleaver, and a hollow turnip lying at his feet! Unable to understand this curious transformation, he clutched the placard with feverish haste, and there, in the grey morning light, he read these fearful words:—

YE OTIS GHOSTE

Ye Onlie True and Originale Spook,

Beware of Ye Imitationes.

All others are counterfeite.

The whole thing flashed across him. He had been tricked, foiled, and out-witted! The old Canterville look came into his eyes; he ground his toothless gums together; and, raising his withered hands high above his head, swore according to the picturesque phraseology of the antique school, that, when Chanticleer had sounded twice his merry horn, deeds of blood would be wrought, and murder walk abroad with silent feet.

Hardly had he finished this awful oath when, from the red-tiled roof of a distant homestead, a cock crew. He laughed a long, low, bitter laugh, and waited. Hour after hour he waited, but the cock, for some strange reason, did not crow again. Finally, at half-past seven, the arrival of the housemaids made him give up his fearful vigil, and he stalked back to his room, thinking of his vain oath and baffled purpose. There he consulted several books of ancient chivalry, of which he was exceedingly fond, and found that, on every occasion on which this oath had been used, Chanticleer had always crowed a second time. "Perdition seize the naughty fowl," he muttered, "I have seen the day when, with my stout spear, I would have run him through the gorge, and made him crow for me an 'twere in death!" He then retired to a comfortable lead coffin, and stayed there till evening.

THINK AND INK...

Questions :

1. Does Mr. Otis have a soft corner for the ghost? Why/why not?

2. Why did Virginia keep away from all the jokes about the ghost? Do you think she is speculative?

3. What actually was the ghost enraged with?

4. What opinion do you form about Mrs. Otis by the way she encountered the ghost?

5. Comment on the ghost facing another ghost.

6. If you had been a member of the Otis family, how would you react to a ghost?

Text-based questions :

1. Why was Mr. Otis annoyed? Do you justify his act?

2. What changes did the Otis family find on the bloodstain?

3. How did these changes amuse the family?

4. What was Virginia's reaction ?

5. How did the ghost appear on a Sunday night?

6. How was the ghost cornered?

7. How was the demoniac laughter of the ghost useful in the previous occasions?

8. What effect did the laughter have on Mrs. Otis?

9. Why did the ghost break down?

10. What was the significance of the armour?

11. What weather did the ghost love?

12. What was his plan for the night?

13. Why did the ghost bear a grudge against Mr. Otis?

14. Describe the horrible spectre that the ghost had in front of him.

15. How did he react on finding another ghost?

16. What made the Canterville ghost to decide upon befriending the other ghost? How was it disappointed later?

17. How was the ghost tricked?

18. Why was the ghost's oath in vain and his purpose baffling?

Vocabulary :

1. Annoyed – irritated
2. Barred – shut
3. Excited – gave rise to
4. Vermillion – bright red colour
5. Kaleidoscopic – colourful
6. Distressed – bothered
7. Acute – severe
8. Agony – sadness
9. Pellets – small metal balls
10. Attained – achieved'
11. Etiquette – good manners
12. Manner – way
13. Shriek – cry
14. Rage – anger
15. Extinguishing – putting out
16. Demoniac – demon like
17. Vaulted – arched

18. Tincture – medicine

19. Glared – looked sharply

20. Fury – anger

21. Renowned – well-known

22. Attributed – recognised

23. Idiocy – stupidity

24. Faintly – slightly

25. Phosphorescent – glowing

26. Vanished – disappeared

27. Vulgarity – rudeness

28. Materialism – worldliness

29. Spectre – ghost

30. Armour – arms, weapons

31. Whiled – spent

32. Weary – sleepy

33. Complimented – praised

34. Casque – headgear

35. Bruising – staining

36. Knuckles – the finger joints

37. Dagger – knife

38. Rattled – upset

39. Gibber – c chatter

40. Grudge – ill-will

41. Reckless – careless

42. Foolhardy – foolish

43. Abject – hopeless

44. Clammy – slippery
45. Charnel-house – place where dead bodies are piled
46. Grabble – to hold
47. Counterpane – bed sheet
48. Palsy – diseased
49. Twitching – trembling
50. Determined – resolute
51. Stifling – breathlessness
52. Corpse – dead body
53. Bleached – made pale
54. Gaiety – joy
55. Sallied – moved suddenly
56. Raven – a bird
57. Croaked – crowed
58. Moaning – crying
59. Stealthily – secretly
60. Wainscoting – wooden panelling
61. Oriel a window structure
62. Blazoned – painted
63. Azure – blue
64. Glided – moved
65. Loathe – hate
66. Baying – howling
67. Anon – soon
68. Brandishing – waving
69. Grotesque – horrible

70. Fantastic – unreal
71. Shroud – covered
72. Chuckled – laughed
73. Blanched – pale
74. Carven – carved
75. Burnished – shine
76. Hideous – ugly
77. Writhed – twisted
78. Eternal – for ever
79. Grin – smile
80. Scarlet – red
81. Swathed – covered
82. Titan – huge
83. Falchion – sword
84. Hasty – fat
85. Glance – look
86. Asserted – assured
87. Grisly – frightening
88. Recumbent – bent
89. Cleaver – broad bladed knife
90. Foiled – prevented
91. Out-witted – out-smarted
92. withered – dried
93. Picturesque – picture like
94. Phraseology – phrase
95. Wrought – created

96. Vigil – watch
97. Stalked – followed
98. Baffled – confused
99. Chivalry – knights, noblemen, horsemen, collectively
100. Perdition - eternal death
101. Muttered - murmured
102. Seize - grab
103. Stout - big
104. Gorge - abyss

Chapter 4

The next day the ghost was very weak and tired. The terrible excitement of the last four weeks was beginning to have its effect. His nerves were completely shattered, and he started at the slightest noise. For five days he kept his room, and at last made up his mind to give up the point of the blood-stain on the library floor. If the Otis family did not want it, they clearly did not deserve it. They were evidently people on a low, material plane of existence, and quite incapable of appreciating the symbolic value of sensuous phenomena. The question of phantasmic apparitions, and the development of astral bodies, was of course quite a different matter, and really not under his control. It was his solemn duty to appear in the corridor once a week, and to gibber from the large oriel window on the first and third Wednesdays in every month, and he did not see how he could honourably escape from his obligations. It is quite true that his life had been very evil, but, upon the other hand, he was most conscientious in all things connected with the supernatural. For the next three Saturdays, accordingly, he traversed the corridor as usual between midnight and three o'clock, taking every possible precaution against being either heard or seen. He removed his boots, trod as lightly as possible on the old worm-eaten boards, wore a large black velvet cloak, and was careful to use the Rising Sun Lubricator for oiling his chains. I am bound to acknowledge that it was with a good deal of difficulty that

"HE MET WITH A SEVERE FALL"

he brought himself to adopt this last mode of protection. However, one night, while the family were at dinner, he slipped into Mr. Otis's bedroom and carried off the bottle. He felt a little humiliated at first, but afterwards was sensible enough to see that there was a great deal to be said for the invention, and, to a certain degree, it served his purpose. Still in spite of everything he was not left unmolested. Strings were continually being stretched across the corridor, over which he tripped in the dark, and on one occasion, while dressed for the part of "Black Isaac, or the Huntsman of

Hogley Woods," he met with a severe fall, through treading on a butter-slide, which the twins had constructed from the entrance of the Tapestry Chamber to the top of the oak staircase. This last insult so enraged him, that he resolved to make one final effort to assert his dignity and social position, and determined to visit the insolent young Etonians the next night in his celebrated character of "Reckless Rupert, or the Headless Earl."

He had not appeared in this disguise for more than seventy years; in fact, not since he had so frightened pretty Lady Barbara Modish by means of it, that she suddenly broke off her engagement with the present Lord Canterville's grandfather, and ran away to Gretna Green with handsome Jack Castletown, declaring that nothing in the world would induce her to marry into a family that allowed such a horrible phantom to walk up and down the terrace at twilight. Poor Jack was afterwards shot in a duel by Lord Canterville on Wandsworth Common, and Lady Barbara died of a broken heart at Tunbridge Wells before the year was out, so, in every way, it had been a great success. It was, however an extremely difficult "make-up," if I may use such a theatrical expression in connection with one of the greatest mysteries of the supernatural, or, to employ a more scientific term, the higher-natural world, and it took him fully three hours to make his preparations. At last everything was ready, and he was very pleased with his appearance. The big leather riding-boots that went with the dress were just a little too large for him, and he could only find one of the two horse-pistols, but, on the whole, he was quite satisfied, and at a quarter-past one he glided out of the wainscoting and crept down the corridor. On reaching the room occupied by the twins, which I should mention was called the Blue Bed Chamber, on account of the colour of its hangings, he found the door just ajar. Wishing to make an effective entrance, he flung it wide

"A HEAVY JUG OF WATER FELL RIGHT DOWN ON HIM."

open, when a heavy jug of water fell right down on him, wetting him to the skin, and just missing his left shoulder by a couple of inches. At the same moment he heard stifled shrieks of laughter proceeding from the four-post bed. The shock to his nervous system was so great that he fled back to his room as hard as he could go, and the next day he was laid up with a severe cold. The only thing that at all consoled him in the whole affair was the fact that he had not brought his head with him, for, had he done so, the consequences might have been very serious.

He now gave up all hope of ever frightening this rude American family, and contented himself, as a rule, with creeping about the passages in list slippers, with a thick red muffler round his throat for fear of draughts, and a small arquebuse, in case he should be attacked by the twins. The final blow he received occurred on the 19th of September. He had gone down-stairs to the great entrance-hall, feeling sure that there, at any rate, he would be quite unmolested, and was amusing himself by making satirical remarks on the large Saroni photographs of the United States Minister and his wife which had now taken the place of the Canterville family pictures. He was simply but neatly clad in a long shroud, spotted with churchyard mould, had tied up his jaw with a strip of yellow

**"MAKING SATIRICAL REMARKS ON THE
PHOTOGRAPHS"**

linen, and carried a small lantern and a sexton's spade. In fact, he was dressed for the character of "Jonas the Graveless, or the Corpse-Snatcher of Chertsey Barn," one of his most remarkable impersonations, and one which the Cantervilles had every reason to remember, as it was the real origin of their quarrel with their neighbour, Lord Rufford. It was about a quarter-past two o'clock in the morning, and, as far as he could ascertain, no one was stirring. As he was strolling towards the library, however, to see if there were any traces left of the blood-stain, suddenly there leaped out on him from a dark corner two figures, who waved their arms wildly above their heads, and shrieked out "BOO!" in his ear.

Seized with a panic, which, under the circumstances, was only natural, he rushed for the staircase, but found Washington Otis waiting for him there with the big garden-syringe, and being thus hemmed in by his enemies on every side, and driven almost to bay, he vanished into the great iron stove, which, fortunately for him, was not lit, and had to make his way home through the flues and chimneys, arriving at his own room in a terrible state of dirt, disorder, and despair.

"SUDDENLY THERE LEAPED OUT TWO FIGURES."

After this he was not seen again on any nocturnal expedition. The twins lay in wait for him on several occasions, and strewed the passages with nutshells every night to the great annoyance of their parents and the servants, but it was of no avail. It was quite evident that his feelings were so wounded that he would not appear. Mr. Otis consequently resumed his great work on the history of the Democratic Party, on which he had been engaged for some years; Mrs. Otis organized a wonderful clam-bake, which amazed the whole county; the boys took to lacrosse euchre, poker, and other American national games, and Virginia rode about the lanes on her pony, accompanied by the young Duke of Cheshire, who had come to spend the last week of his holidays at Canterville Chase. It was generally assumed that the ghost had gone away, and, in fact, Mr. Otis wrote a letter to that effect to Lord Canterville, who, in reply, expressed his great pleasure at the news, and sent his best congratulations to the Minister's worthy wife.

The Otises, however, were deceived, for the ghost was still in the house, and though now almost an invalid, was by no means ready to let matters rest, particularly as he heard that among the guests was the young Duke of Cheshire, whose grand-uncle, Lord Francis Stilton, had once bet a hundred guineas with Colonel Carbury that he would play dice with the Canterville ghost, and was found the next morning lying on the floor of the card-room in such a helpless paralytic state that, though he lived on to a great age, he was never able to say anything again but "Double Sixes." The story was well known at the time, though, of course, out of respect to the feelings of the two noble families, every attempt was made to hush it up, and a full account of all the circumstances connected with it will be found in the third volume of Lord Tattle's Recollections of the Prince Regent and his Friends. The ghost, then, was naturally very anxious to show that he had not lost his influence over the Stiltons, with whom, indeed, he was distantly connected, his own first cousin having been married *en secondes noces* to the Sieur de Bulkeley, from whom, as every one knows, the Dukes of Cheshire are lineally descended. Accordingly, he made arrangements for appearing to Virginia's little lover in his celebrated impersonation of "The Vampire Monk, or the Bloodless Benedictine," a performance so horrible that when old Lady Startup saw it, which she did on one fatal New Year's Eve, in the year 1764, she went off into the most piercing shrieks, which culminated in violent apoplexy, and died in three days, after disinheriting the Cantervilles, who were her nearest relations, and leaving all her money to her London apothecary. At the last moment, however, his terror of the twins prevented his leaving his room, and the little Duke slept in peace under the great feathered canopy in the Royal Bedchamber, and dreamed of Virginia.

THINK AND INK...

Questions :

1. Considering the happenings, was the ghost heading towards a failure in his nocturnal expeditions?

2. What , according to the ghost, was the symbolic value of sensuous phenomena?

3. Were the twins handling the ghost the right way?

4. In what way should the ghost teach a lesson to the twins?

5. What finally despaired the ghost ?

6. Why, do you think, did the ghost continue to stay in the house in spite of all his failed attempts to frighten the Otis's? family ?

Text-based questions :

1. Describe the condition of the ghost after his bitter experiences.

2. What were the obligations of the ghost ?

3. Why was there a 'good deal of difficulty' for the ghost to protect himself from the Otis family?

4. How did the ghost surrender to Mr. Otis?

5. How was the ghost's character of 'Reckless Rupert or the Headless Earl' received by the inmates?

6. What efforts did the ghost make to make his disguise perfect, and how were his efforts failed?

7. What final blow did the ghost receive on the 19th of September?

8. How was the ghost hemmed in by his enemies?

9. How was the Otis family deceived?

10. What was the experience of Lord Francis Stilton with the Canterville ghost?

11. How horrible was the 'Vampire Monk"?

12. Why did the ghost give up his attempt to terrify the Duke?

13. What changes did the absence of the ghost bring about in the family? Why?

Vocabulary :

1. Excitement - disturbance

2. Shattered - horrified

3. Started - moved

4. Sensuous - intense

5. Apparitions - ghosts

6. Astral - astronomical

7. Solemn - serious

8. Obligations - duties

9. Conscientious - careful

10. Supernatural - ghostly

11. Traversed - went across

12. Humiliated - shamed

13. Unmolested - untroubled

14. Tripped - fell

15. Enraged - angered

16. Dignity - status

17. Insolent- ill-mannered

18. Earl - a British nobleman

19. Disguise - costume

20. Induce - compel

21. Twilight - dawn and dusk

22. Theatrical - dramatic

23. Consequences - results

24. Contented - satisfied

25. Creeping - moving secretly

26. Draughts - cold breeze

27. Arquebuse - rifle

28. Satirical -critical

29. Shroud - cover for a dead body

30. Sextons - those in charge of the charge

31. Remarkable - notable

32. Impersonations - imitations

33. Ascertain - assure

34. Strolling - walking

35. Panic - fear

36. Hemmed - surrounded

37. Flues - ducts for smoke

38. Nocturnal - of the night

39. Expedition - trips

40. Strewed - scattered

41. Larosse euchre - a game

42. Deceived - cheated

43. Invalid - worthless

44. Guineas - currency

45. Paralytic - paralysis

46. Hush up - cover up

47. Circumstances - situationsanzious - eager

48. Influence - authority

49. Lineally - in the line of

50. Vampire - a bloodsucker

51. Benedictine - a monk

52. Piercing - painful

53. Culminated - ended

54. Apothecary - a pharmacist

55. Canopy - a cloth cover

Chapter 5

A few days after this, Virginia and her curly-haired cavalier went out riding on Brockley meadows, where she tore her habit so badly in getting through a hedge that, on their return home, she made up her mind to go up by the back staircase so as not to be seen. As she was running past the Tapestry Chamber, the door of which happened to be open, she fancied she saw some one inside, and thinking it was her mother's maid, who sometimes used to bring her work there, looked in to ask her to mend her habit. To her immense surprise, however, it was the Canterville Ghost himself! He was sitting by the window, watching the ruined gold of the yellowing trees fly through the air, and the red leaves dancing madly down the long avenue. His head was leaning on his hand, and his whole attitude was one of extreme depression. Indeed, so forlorn, and so much out of repair did he look, that little Virginia, whose first idea had been to run away and lock herself in her room, was filled with pity, and determined to try and comfort him. So light was her footfall, and so deep his melancholy, that he was not aware of her presence till she spoke to him.

"I am so sorry for you," she said, "but my brothers are going back to Eton to-morrow, and then, if you behave yourself, no one will annoy you."

"It is absurd asking me to behave myself," he answered, looking round in astonishment at the pretty little girl who had ventured to address him, "quite absurd. I must rattle my chains, and groan through keyholes, and walk about at night, if that is what you mean. It is my only reason for existing."

"It is no reason at all for existing, and you know you have been very wicked. Mrs. Umney told us, the first day we arrived here, that you had killed your wife."

"Well, I quite admit it," said the Ghost, petulantly, "but it was a purely family matter, and concerned no one else."

"It is very wrong to kill any one," said Virginia, who at times had a sweet puritan gravity, caught from some old New England ancestor.

"Oh, I hate the cheap severity of abstract ethics! My wife was very plain, never had my ruffs properly starched, and knew nothing about cookery. Why, there was a buck I had shot in Hogley Woods, a magnificent pricket, and do you know how she had it sent to table? However, it is no matter now, for it is all over, and I don't think it was very nice of her brothers to starve me to death, though I did kill her."

"Starve you to death? Oh, Mr. Ghost—I mean Sir Simon, are you hungry? I have a sandwich in my case. Would you like it?"

"No, thank you, I never eat anything now; but it is very kind of you, all the same, and you are much nicer than the rest of your horrid, rude, vulgar, dishonest family."

"Stop!" cried Virginia, stamping her foot, "it is you who are rude, and horrid, and vulgar, and as for dishonesty, you know you stole the paints out of my box to try and furbish up that ridiculous blood-stain in the library. First you took all my reds, including the vermilion, and I couldn't do any more sunsets, then you took the emerald-green and the chrome-yellow, and finally I had nothing left but indigo and Chinese white, and could only do moonlight scenes, which are always depressing to look at, and not at all easy to paint. I never told on you, though I was very much annoyed, and it was most ridiculous, the whole thing; for who ever heard of emerald-green blood?"

"Well, really," said the Ghost, rather meekly, "what was I to do? It is a very difficult thing to get real blood nowadays, and, as your brother began it all with his Paragon Detergent, I certainly saw no reason why I should not have your paints. As for colour, that is always a matter of taste: the Cantervilles have blue blood, for instance, the very bluest in England; but I know you Americans don't care for things of this kind."

"You know nothing about it, and the best thing you can do is to emigrate and improve your mind. My father will be only too happy to give you a free passage, and though there is a heavy duty on spirits of every kind, there will be no difficulty about the Custom House, as the officers are all Democrats. Once in New York, you are sure to be a great success. I know lots of people there who would give a hundred thousand dollars to have a grandfather, and much more than that to have a family ghost."

"I don't think I should like America."

"I suppose because we have no ruins and no curiosities," said Virginia, satirically.

"No ruins! no curiosities!" answered the Ghost; "you have your navy and your manners."

"Good evening; I will go and ask papa to get the twins an extra week's holiday."

"Please don't go, Miss Virginia," he cried; "I am so lonely and so unhappy, and I really don't know what to do. I want to go to sleep and I cannot."

"That's quite absurd! You have merely to go to bed and blow out the candle. It is very difficult sometimes to keep awake, especially at church, but there is no difficulty at all about sleeping. Why, even babies know how to do that, and they are not very clever."

"I have not slept for three hundred years," he said sadly, and Virginia's beautiful blue eyes opened in wonder; "for three hundred years I have not slept, and I am so tired."

Virginia grew quite grave, and her little lips trembled like rose-leaves. She came towards him, and kneeling down at his side, looked up into his old withered face.

"Poor, poor Ghost," she murmured; "have you no place where you can sleep?"

"'POOR, POOR GHOST,' SHE MURMURED; 'HAVE YOU NO PLACE WHERE YOU CAN SLEEP?'"

"Far away beyond the pine-woods," he answered, in a low, dreamy voice, "there is a little garden. There the grass grows long and deep, there are the great white stars of the hemlock flower, there the nightingale sings all night long. All night long he sings, and the cold crystal moon looks down, and the yew-tree spreads out its giant arms over the sleepers."

Virginia's eyes grew dim with tears, and she hid her face in her hands.

"You mean the Garden of Death," she whispered.

"Yes, death. Death must be so beautiful. To lie in the soft brown earth, with the grasses waving above one's head, and listen to silence. To have no yesterday, and no to-morrow. To forget time, to forget life, to be at peace. You can help me. You can open for me the portals of death's house, for love is always with you, and love is stronger than death is."

Virginia trembled, a cold shudder ran through her, and for a few moments there was silence. She felt as if she was in a terrible dream.

Then the ghost spoke again, and his voice sounded like the sighing of the wind.

"Have you ever read the old prophecy on the library window?"

"Oh, often," cried the little girl, looking up; "I know it quite well. It is painted in curious black letters, and is difficult to read. There are only six lines:

> "*When a golden girl can win*
> *Prayer from out the lips of sin,*
> *When the barren almond bears,*
> *And a little child gives away its tears,*
> *Then shall all the house be still*
> *And peace come to Canterville.*'

"But I don't know what they mean."

"They mean," he said, sadly, "that you must weep with me for my sins, because I have no tears, and pray with me for my soul, because I have no faith, and then, if you have always been sweet, and good, and gentle, the angel of death will have mercy on me. You will see fearful shapes in darkness, and wicked voices will whisper in your ear, but they will not harm you, for against the purity of a little child the powers of Hell cannot prevail."

Virginia made no answer, and the ghost wrung his hands in wild despair as he looked down at her bowed golden head. Suddenly she stood up, very pale, and with a strange light in her eyes. "I am not afraid," she said firmly, "and I will ask the angel to have mercy on you."

He rose from his seat with a faint cry of joy, and taking her hand bent over it with old-fashioned grace and kissed it. His fingers were as cold as ice, and his lips burned like fire, but Virginia did not falter, as he led her across the dusky room. On the faded green tapestry were broidered little huntsmen. They blew their tasselled horns and with their tiny hands waved to her to go back. "Go back! little Virginia," they cried, "go back!" but the ghost clutched her hand more tightly, and she shut her eyes against them. Horrible animals with lizard tails and goggle eyes blinked at her from the carven chimneypiece, and murmured, "Beware! little Virginia, beware! we may never see you again," but the Ghost glided on more swiftly, and Virginia did not listen. When they reached the end of the room he stopped, and muttered some words she could not understand. She opened her eyes, and saw the wall slowly fading away like a mist, and a great black cavern in front of her. A bitter cold wind swept round them, and she felt something pulling at her dress. "Quick, quick," cried the Ghost, "or it will be too late," and in a moment the wainscoting had closed behind them, and the Tapestry Chamber was empty.

"THE GHOST GLIDED ON MORE SWIFTLY"

THINK AND INK...

Questions :

1. Considering her nature, should Virginia be frightened on seeing the ghost? Explain.

2. Did Virginia handle the ghost the right way? Why/why not?

3. What do you understand about Virginia from the circumstances you find her in?

4. Is the ghost right in killing his wife?

5. What did the ghost want from Virginia?

6. Why did Virginia want to help the ghost?

7. Why did Virginia find death beautiful? Was it one of the ways to convince the ghost?

8. What did the old prophecy on the library window predict?

9. Who could be the little girl that the prophecy referred to ?

10. Was the ghost ready to go to the garden of death? Why/why not?

11. Why did the ghost choose Virginia to weep for his sins?

12. The ghost who had been haunting the house for three hundred years, decided to go to the garden of death if Virginia goes with him. What does this prove?

13. Comment on the nature of Virginia as reflected in her consoling and convincing of the ghost.

14. What made Virginia say that she would ask the angel to forgive the ghost?

15. Who were the little huntsmen, and why did they try to stop Virginia?

16. Why didn't Virginia listen to the huntsmen? What was her real intention?

17. Analyse Virginia's decision to leave the ghost in the garden of death.

Text-based Questions :

1. What happened when Virginia went out with her cavalier?

2. Who did she meet inside the tapestry chamber?

3. How was the ghost looking?

4. Why did Virginia feel sorry for the ghost?

5. How did Virginia convince the ghost that there is no reason for him to exist?

6. What reason did the ghost give for killing his wife?

7. What accusations did Virginia throw upon the ghost?

8. How does the Garden of Death look?

9. Why did Virginia say that death must be beautiful?

10. What did the ghost request Virginia? And why did she concede to his request?

11. Where was Virginia taken by the ghost? Describe the pathway where she was taken by the ghost.

12. What happened when they reached the end of the room?

Vocabulary :

1. Cavalier - a soldier riding a horse

2. Hedge - grassy laws

3. Made up her mind - decided

4. Fancied - imagined

5. Immense - great

6. Ruined - destroyed

7. Attitude - manner

8. Depression - sadness

9. Determined - firm

10. Footfall - footsteps

11. Absurd - illogical

12. Astonishment - surprise

13. Ventured -dared

14. Rattle - clatter

15. Wicked - bad

16. Puritan - strict about religion

17. Gravity - seriousness

18. Severity - strictness

19. Abstract - vague

20. Ruffs - frills

21. Pricket - a buck in its second year

22. Starve - be hungry

23. Furbish - renovate

24. Instance - (here. example

25. Emigrate - go out of country

26. Passage - movement

27. Curiosities - strange things

28. Grave - serious

29. Trembled - shivered

30. Dreamy - faraway

31. Hemlock - poisonous plant

32. Giant - huge

33. Shudder - tremble

34. Sighing - noisy

35. Prophecy - prediction, tell about future

36. Barren - empty

37. Soul - the spirit

38. Whisper - murmur
39. Prevail - overcome
40. Falter - stop
41. Dusky - dark
42. Broidered - embroider
43. Tasselled - bundle of thread tied together at on end
44. Waved - signalled
45. Clutched - held'
46. Blinked - winked, open and close the eye
47. Murmured - talk softly
48. Beware - be aware of
49. Swiftly - quickly
50. Muttered - said
51. Fading - becoming weak
52. Cavern - cave
53. Swept - cleared

Chapter 6

About ten minutes later, the bell rang for tea, and, as Virginia did not come down, Mrs. Otis sent up one of the footmen to tell her. After a little time he returned and said that he could not find Miss Virginia anywhere. As she was in the habit of going out to the garden every evening to get flowers for the dinner-table, Mrs. Otis was not at all alarmed at first, but when six o'clock struck, and Virginia did not appear, she became really agitated, and sent the boys out to look for her, while she herself and Mr. Otis searched every room in the house. At half-past six the boys came back and said that they could find no trace of their sister anywhere. They were all now in the greatest state of excitement, and did not know what to do, when Mr. Otis suddenly remembered that, some few days before, he had given a band of gipsies permission to camp in the park. He accordingly at once set off for Blackfell Hollow, where he knew they were, accompanied by his eldest son and two of the farm-servants. The little Duke of Cheshire, who was perfectly frantic with anxiety, begged hard to be allowed to go too, but Mr. Otis would not allow him, as he was afraid there might be a scuffle. On arriving at the spot, however, he found that the gipsies had gone, and it was evident that their departure had been rather sudden, as the fire was still burning, and some plates were lying on the grass. Having sent off Washington and the two men to scour the district, he ran home, and despatched telegrams to all the police inspectors in the county, telling them to look out for a little girl who had been kidnapped by tramps or gipsies. He then ordered his horse to be brought round, and, after insisting on his wife and the three boys sitting down to dinner, rode off down the Ascot road with a groom. He had hardly, however, gone a couple of miles, when he heard somebody galloping after him, and, looking round, saw the little Duke coming up on his pony, with his face very flushed, and no hat. "I'm awfully sorry, Mr. Otis," gasped out the boy, "but I can't eat any dinner as long as Virginia is lost. Please don't be angry with me; if you had let us be engaged last year, there would never have been all this trouble. You won't send me back, will you? I can't go! I won't go!"

"HE HEARD SOMEBODY GALLOPING AFTER HIM"

The Minister could not help smiling at the handsome young scapegrace, and was a good deal touched at his devotion to Virginia, so leaning down from his horse, he patted him kindly on the shoulders, and said, "Well, Cecil, if you won't go back, I suppose you must come with me, but I must get you a hat at Ascot."

"Oh, bother my hat! I want Virginia!" cried the little Duke, laughing, and they galloped on to the railway station. There Mr. Otis inquired of the station-master if any one answering to the description of Virginia had been seen on the platform, but could get no news of her. The station-master, however, wired up and down the line, and assured him that a strict watch would be kept for her, and, after having bought a hat for the little Duke from a linen-draper, who was just putting up his shutters, Mr. Otis rode off to Bexley, a village about four miles away, which he was told was a well-known haunt of the gipsies, as there was a large common next to it. Here they roused up the rural policeman, but could get no information from him, and, after riding all over the common, they turned their horses' heads homewards, and reached the Chase about eleven o'clock, dead-tired and almost heart-broken. They found Washington and the twins waiting for them at the gate-house with lanterns, as the avenue was very dark. Not the slightest trace of Virginia had been discovered. The gipsies had been caught on Brockley meadows, but she was not with them, and they had explained their sudden departure by saying that they had mistaken the date of Chorton Fair, and had gone off in a hurry for fear they should be late. Indeed, they had been quite distressed at hearing of Virginia's disappearance, as they were very grateful to Mr. Otis for having allowed them to camp in his park, and four of their number had stayed behind to help in the search. The carp-pond had been dragged, and the whole Chase thoroughly gone over, but without any result. It was evident that, for that night at any rate, Virginia was lost to them; and it was in a state of the deepest depression that Mr. Otis and the boys walked up to the house, the groom following behind with the two horses and the pony. In the hall they found a group of frightened servants, and lying on a sofa in the library was poor Mrs. Otis, almost out of her mind with terror and anxiety, and having her forehead bathed with eau de cologne by the old housekeeper. Mr. Otis at once insisted on her having something to eat, and ordered up supper for the whole party. It was a melancholy meal, as hardly any one spoke, and even the twins were awestruck and subdued, as they were very fond of their sister. When they had finished, Mr. Otis, in spite of the entreaties of the little Duke, ordered them all to bed, saying that nothing more could be done that night, and that he would telegraph in the morning to Scotland Yard for some detectives to be sent down immediately. Just as they were passing out of the dining-room, midnight began to boom from the clock tower, and when the last stroke sounded they heard a crash and a sudden shrill cry; a dreadful peal of thunder shook the house, a strain of unearthly music floated through the air, a panel at the top of the staircase flew back with a loud noise, and out on the landing, looking very pale and white, with a little casket in her hand, stepped Virginia. In a moment they had all rushed up to her. Mrs. Otis clasped her passionately in her arms, the Duke smothered her with violent kisses, and the twins executed a wild war-dance round the group.

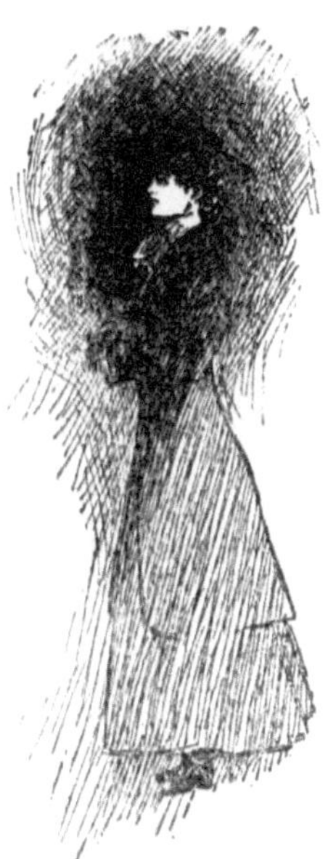

"OUT ON THE LANDING STEPPED VIRGINIA"

"Good heavens! child, where have you been?" said Mr. Otis, rather angrily, thinking that she had been playing some foolish trick on them. "Cecil and I have been riding all over the country looking for you, and your mother has been frightened to death. You must never play these practical jokes any more."

"Except on the Ghost! except on the Ghost!" shrieked the twins, as they capered about.

"My own darling, thank God you are found; you must never leave my side again," murmured Mrs. Otis, as she kissed the trembling child, and smoothed the tangled gold of her hair.

"Papa," said Virginia, quietly, "I have been with the Ghost. He is dead, and you must come and see him. He had been very wicked, but he was really sorry for all that he had done, and he gave me this box of beautiful jewels before he died."

The whole family gazed at her in mute amazement, but she was quite grave and serious; and, turning round, she led them through the opening in the wainscoting down a narrow secret corridor, Washington following with a lighted candle, which he had caught up from the table. Finally, they came to a great oak door, studded with rusty nails. When Virginia touched it, it swung back on its heavy hinges, and they found themselves in a little low room, with a vaulted ceiling, and one tiny grated window. Imbedded in the wall was a huge iron ring, and chained to it was a gaunt skeleton, that was stretched out at full length on the stone floor, and seemed to be trying to grasp with its long fleshless fingers an old-fashioned trencher and ewer, that were placed just out of its reach. The jug had evidently been once filled with water, as it was covered inside with green mould. There was nothing on the trencher but a pile of dust. Virginia knelt down beside the skeleton, and, folding her little hands together, began to pray silently, while the rest of the party looked on in wonder at the terrible tragedy whose secret was now disclosed to them.

"CHAINED TO IT WAS A GAUNT SKELETON"

"Hallo!" suddenly exclaimed one of the twins, who had been looking out of the window to try and discover in what wing of the house the room was situated. "Hallo! the old withered almond-tree has blossomed. I can see the flowers quite plainly in the moonlight."

"God has forgiven him," said Virginia, gravely, as she rose to her feet, and a beautiful light seemed to illumine her face.

"What an angel you are!" cried the young Duke, and he put his arm round her neck, and kissed her.

THINK AND INK...

Questions :

1. Is the Duke truly in love with Virginia? How do you say?

2. What did the Virginia family presume when they found Virginia missing?

3. What could be the real reason for Mrs. Otis's fear?

4. Where had Virginia been all the while? How do you say?

5. Was Otis family happy and convinced about the death of the ghost? Give reasons in support of your answer.

6. What qualities of Virginia do you find that made her angelic?

7. Why was Mrs. Otis's mind filled with terror and anxiety at the disappearance of her daughter, considering her strong will power?

Text based questions :

1. What was the family excited about?

2. Who and why did Mr. Otis suspect at first for the disappearance of Virginia?

3. How was he disappointed finally?

4. How did the Duke exhibit his devotion to Virginia?

5. How was the family depressed?

6. What happened when the last stroke sounded?

7. How did Virginia look as she come back?

8. What did she tell her family?

9. Where did she take her family? And what did she show them there?

10. How did the twins express their delight at the death of the ghost?

Vocabulary :

1. Footmen - servants
2. Alarmed - shocked
3. Agitated - disturbed
4. Excitement -tension
5. Gypsies - travelling traders
6. Accompanied - went along with
7. Frantic - hysterical, worried
8. Anxiety - worry
9. Evident- clear
10. Departure - leave
11. Scour - search
12. Tramps
13. Insisting - compelling
14. Flushed - red colour
15. Awfully - terribly
16. Scapegrace - rascal
17. Devotion - attachment
18. Leaning - bending
19. Patted - tapped
20. Galloped - ride in a horse
22. Inquired - questioned
22. Avenue - pathway
23. Slightest - least
24. Distressed - troubled
25. Disappearance - going away
26. Grateful - thankful

27. Dragged - pulled
28. Depression - sadness
29. Awestruck - absorbed
30. Subdued - quiet
31. Entreaties - requests
32. Shrill - sharp
33. Dreadful - frightening
34. Unearthly - not from this world
35. Casket - treasure box
36. Capered - jumped
37. Tangled -coiled
38. Amazement - wonderful
39. Corridor - passageway
40. Studded - covered
41. Hinges - handles
42. Grated - grilled
43. Imbedded - fixed
44. Gaunt - thin
45. Trencher - wooden board
46. Ewer - mug
47. Evidently - clearly
48. Beside - next to
49. Disclosed - revealed, opened

Chapter 7

Four days after these curious incidents, a funeral started from Canterville Chase at about eleven o'clock at night. The hearse was drawn by eight black horses, each of which carried on its head a great tuft of nodding ostrich-plumes, and the leaden coffin was

**"BY THE SIDE OF THE HEARSE AND
THE COACHES WALKED THE SERVANTS
WITH LIGHTED TORCHES"**

covered by a rich purple pall, on which was embroidered in gold the Canterville coat-of-arms. By the side of the hearse and the coaches walked the servants with lighted torches, and the whole procession was wonderfully impressive. Lord Canterville was the chief mourner, having come up specially from Wales to attend the funeral, and sat in the first carriage along with little Virginia. Then came the United States Minister and his wife, then Washington and the three boys, and in the last carriage was Mrs. Umney. It was generally felt that, as she had been frightened by the ghost for more than fifty years of her life, she had a right to see the last of him. A deep grave had been dug in the corner of the churchyard, just under the old yew-tree, and the service was read in the most impressive manner by the Rev. Augustus Dampier. When the ceremony was over, the servants, according to an old custom observed in the Canterville family, extinguished their torches, and, as the coffin was being lowered into the grave, Virginia stepped forward, and laid on it a large cross made of white and pink almond-blossoms. As she did so, the moon came out from behind a cloud, and flooded with its silent silver the little churchyard, and from a distant copse a nightingale began to sing. She thought of the ghost's description of the Garden of Death, her eyes became dim with tears, and she hardly spoke a word during the drive home.

THE MOON CAME OUT FROM BEHIND A CLOUD

The next morning, before Lord Canterville went up to town, Mr. Otis had an interview with him on the subject of the jewels the ghost had given to Virginia. They were perfectly magnificent, especially a certain ruby necklace with old Venetian setting, which was really a superb specimen of sixteenth-century work, and their value was so great that Mr. Otis felt considerable scruples about allowing his daughter to accept them.

"My lord," he said, "I know that in this country mortmain is held to apply to trinkets as well as to land, and it is quite clear to me that these jewels are, or should be, heirlooms in your family. I must beg you, accordingly, to take them to London with you, and to regard them simply as a portion of your property which has been restored to you under certain strange conditions. As for my daughter, she is merely a child, and has as yet, I am glad to say, but little interest in such appurtenances of idle luxury. I am also informed by Mrs. Otis, who, I may say, is no mean authority upon Art,—having had the privilege of spending several winters in Boston when she was a girl,—that these gems are of great monetary worth, and if offered for sale would fetch a tall price. Under these circumstances, Lord Canterville, I feel sure that you will recognize how impossible it would be for me to allow them to remain in the possession of any member of my family; and, indeed, all such vain gauds and toys, however suitable or necessary to the dignity of the British aristocracy, would be completely out of place among those who have been brought up on the severe, and I believe immortal, principles of Republican simplicity. Perhaps I should mention that Virginia is very anxious that you should allow her to retain the box, as a memento of your unfortunate but misguided ancestor. As it is extremely old, and consequently a good deal out of repair, you may perhaps think fit to comply with her request. For my own part, I confess I am a good deal surprised to find a child of mine expressing sympathy with mediævalism in any form, and can only account for it by the fact that Virginia was born in one of your London suburbs shortly after Mrs. Otis had returned from a trip to Athens."

Lord Canterville listened very gravely to the worthy Minister's speech, pulling his grey moustache now and then to hide an involuntary smile, and when Mr. Otis had ended, he shook him cordially by the hand, and said: "My dear sir, your charming little daughter rendered my unlucky ancestor, Sir Simon, a very important service, and I and my family are much indebted to her for her marvellous courage and pluck. The jewels are clearly hers, and, egad, I believe that if I were heartless enough to take them from her, the wicked old fellow would be out of his grave in a fortnight, leading me the devil of a life. As for their being heirlooms, nothing is an heirloom that is not so mentioned in a will or legal document, and the existence of these jewels has been quite unknown. I assure you I have no more claim on them than your butler, and when Miss Virginia grows up, I dare say she will be pleased to have pretty things to wear. Besides, you forget, Mr. Otis, that you took the furniture and the ghost at a valuation, and anything that belonged to the ghost passed at once into your possession, as, whatever activity Sir Simon may have shown in the corridor at night, in point of law he was really dead, and you acquired his property by purchase."

Mr. Otis was a good deal distressed at Lord Canterville's refusal, and begged him to reconsider his decision, but the good-natured peer was quite firm, and finally induced the Minister to allow his daughter to retain the present the ghost had given her, and when, in the spring of 1890, the young Duchess of Cheshire was presented at the Queen's first drawing-room on the occasion of her marriage, her jewels were the universal theme of admiration. For Virginia received the coronet, which is the reward of all good little American girls, and was married to her boy-lover as soon as he came of age. They were both so charming, and they loved each other so much, that every one was delighted at the match, except the old Marchioness of Dumbleton, who had tried to catch the Duke for one of her seven unmarried daughters, and had given no less than three expensive dinner-parties for that purpose, and, strange to say, Mr. Otis himself. Mr. Otis was extremely fond of the young Duke personally, but, theoretically, he objected to titles, and, to use his own words, "was not without apprehension lest, amid the enervating influences of a pleasure-loving aristocracy, the true principles of Republican simplicity should be forgotten." His objections, however, were completely overruled, and I believe that when he walked up the aisle of St. George's, Hanover Square, with his daughter leaning on his arm, there was not a prouder man in the whole length and breadth of England.

The Duke and Duchess, after the honeymoon was over, went down to Canterville Chase, and on the day after their arrival they walked over in the afternoon to the lonely churchyard by the pine-woods. There had been a great deal of difficulty at first about the inscription on Sir Simon's tombstone, but finally it had been decided to engrave on it simply the initials of the old gentleman's name, and the verse from the library window. The Duchess had brought with her some lovely roses, which she strewed upon the grave, and after they had stood by it for some time they strolled into the ruined chancel of the old abbey. There the Duchess sat down on a fallen pillar, while her husband lay at her feet smoking a cigarette and looking up at her beautiful eyes. Suddenly he threw his cigarette away, took hold of her hand, and said to her, "Virginia, a wife should have no secrets from her husband."

"Dear Cecil! I have no secrets from you."

"Yes, you have," he answered, smiling, "you have never told me what happened to you when you were locked up with the ghost."

"I have never told any one, Cecil," said Virginia, gravely.

"I know that, but you might tell me."

"Please don't ask me, Cecil, I cannot tell you. Poor Sir Simon! I owe him a great deal. Yes, don't laugh, Cecil, I really do. He made me see what Life is, and what Death signifies, and why Love is stronger than both."

The Duke rose and kissed his wife lovingly.

"You can have your secret as long as I have your heart," he murmured.

"You have always had that, Cecil."

"And you will tell our children some day, won't you?"

Virginia blushed.

THINK AND INK...

Questions :

1. Should the ghost be given such a grand funeral. Why/why not?

2. What made Virginia cry at the thought of the description of the ghost about the garden of death?

3. Do you find it right that Mr. Otis wanted to return the jewels to its owners?

4. Throw light on the mutual honesty that you find in Mr. Otis and Lord Canterville (at the beginning of the story and now.?)

5. What contrasting picture of lifestyle does Mr. Otis draw in his conversation with Lord Canterville?

6. In what way did Lord Canterville feel indebted to Virginia?

7. What did Virginia owe to the ghost and do you justify her stand?

Text based questions :

1. Describe the funeral scenery.

2. How was Virginia looking?

3. Why did Mr. Otis want to return the jewels to Lord Canterville?

4. What did Lord Canterville tell Mr. Otis in return?

5. What was the significance of the jewels?

6. Describe the marriage ceremony.

7. Where and why did the Duke and the Duchess go after the honeymoon?

8. What did the Duke want to know from Virginia?

9. Why didn't Virginia share her secret with her husband?

10. Why did she say that she owed a great deal to the ghost?

Vocabulary :

1. Hearse - a carriage that carries the coffin
2. Tuft - cluster of hair
3. Plumes - feathers
4. Leaden - dull, grey
5. Coat-of-arms - the heraldic bearings of a family
6. Impressive - attractive
7. Mourner - one who cries for the dead
8. Carriage - vehicle
9. Extinguished - put out
10. Interview - short conversation
11. Magnificent - grand
12. Specimen - sample
13. Mortmain - legal ownership of land
14. Trinkets - expensive ornaments
15. Heirlooms - ancestral jewels
16. Appurtenances - additions
17. Privilege - benefit, concession
18. Gauds - trinkets
19. Immortal - undying, everlasting
20. Memento - a token of memory
21. Misguided - mistaken
22. Ancestor - forefather
23. Consequently - as a result of
24. Medievalism - of the middle ages
25. Suburbs - outskirts of a city
26. Involuntary - unintentional

27. Charming - beautiful

28. Rendered - made

29. Indebted - grateful

30. Pluck - determination

31. Egad - surprise

32. Heartless - merciless

33. Acquired - obtained

34. Reconsider - rethink

35. Peer - of equal status

36. Induced - persuaded, compelled

37. Universal - worldwide

38. Coronet - crown

39. Delighted - happy

40. Expensive - costly

41. Apprehension - fear

42. Lest - in case

43. Enervating - weakening

44. Aristrocracy - nobility

45. Overruled - overpowered

46. Prouder - feeling great

47. Inscription - words etched on a stone

48. Tombstone - grave

49. Engrave - carve, etch

50. Initials - the first letter

51. Chancel - a part of the church

52. Abbey - a large church

www.ingramcontent.com/pod-product-compliance
Lightning Source LLC
Chambersburg PA
CBHW051255160726
47994CB00003B/1174